Hello, Hedgehog!

Let's Have a Sleepover!

Norm Feuti

🌰 ACORN™
SCHOLASTIC INC.

For Jen —NF

Library of Congress Cataloging-in-Publication Data

Names: Feuti, Norman, author.
Title: Let's have a sleepover! / Norm Feuti.
Description: First edition. | New York, NY : Scholastic Inc., [2019] |
Series: Hello, Hedgehog! ; 2 | Summary: Harry and Hedgehog are having a sleepover, but Harry is uneasy about sleeping outside.
Identifiers: LCCN 2018035385| ISBN 9781338281415 (pbk.) | ISBN 9781338281422 (hardcover)
Subjects: LCSH: Sleepovers—Juvenile fiction. | Tents—Juvenile fiction. |
Best friends—Juvenile fiction. | Friendship—Juvenile fiction. | CYAC:
Sleepovers—Fiction. | Tents—Fiction. | Best friends—Fiction. |
Friendship—Fiction. | Hedgehogs--Fiction.
Classification: LCC PZ7.1.F52 Le 2019 | DDC [E—dc23 LC record available at
LC record available at https://lccn.loc.gov/ 2018035385

10 9 8 7 6 5 4 3 2 1   19 20 21 22 23

Printed in China   62
First edition, September 2019
Edited by Katie Carella
Book design by Maria Mercado

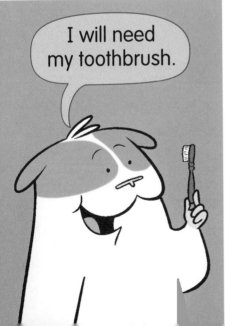

I am too old for teddy bears.

The Tent

19

I brought my blanket.

I brought my toothbrush and my book.

And, um . . .

23

27

33

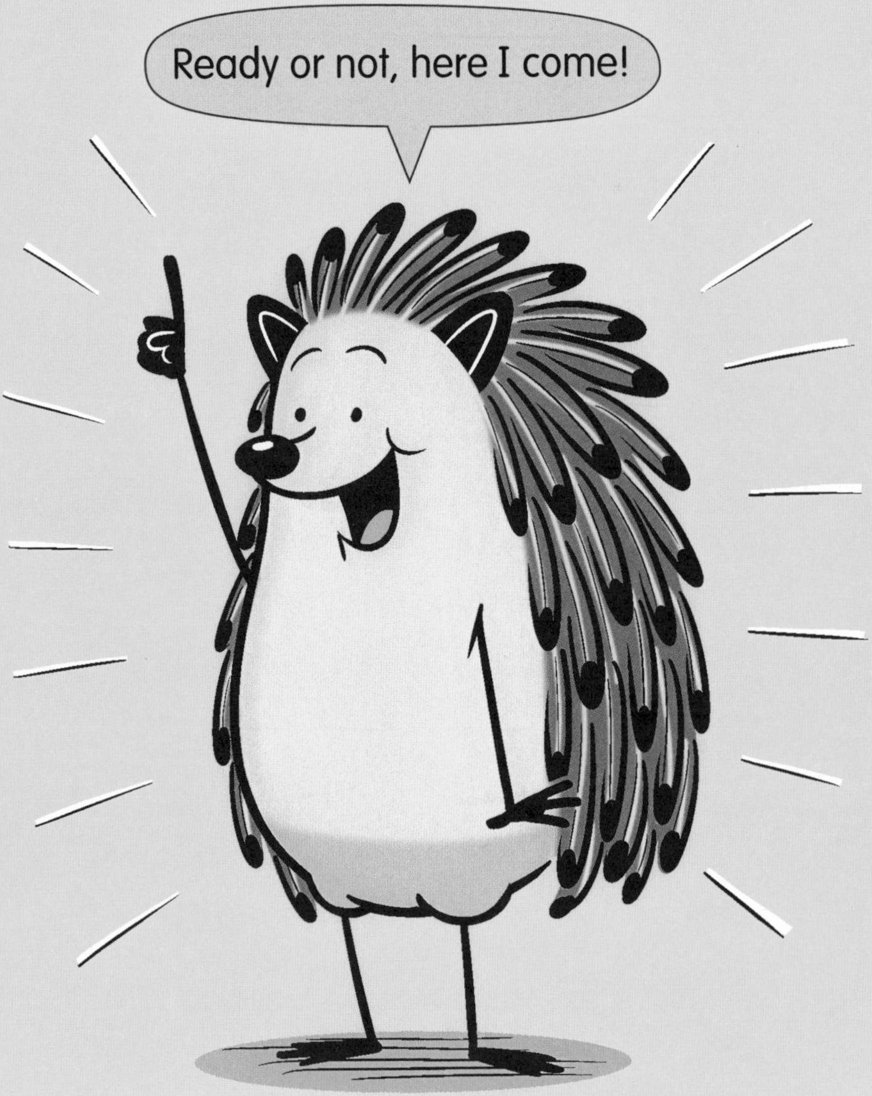
Ready or not, here I come!

43

About the Author

Norm Feuti lives in Massachusetts with his family, a dog, two cats, and a guinea pig. He is the creator of the newspaper comic strips **Retail** and **Gil**. He is also the author and illustrator of the graphic novel **The King of Kazoo**. **Hello, Hedgehog!** is Norm's first early reader series.

YOU CAN DRAW HARRY!

1. Draw a potato shape.

2. Draw the ears, hair, and two big bumps for the mouth!

3. Add legs, feet, and a tail.

4. Draw an arm and a hand.

5. Add eyes, eyebrows, a chin, and a wide letter T for the nose.

6. Color in your drawing!

WHAT'S YOUR STORY?

Harry is sleeping over at Hedgehog's house.
Imagine Hedgehog asks **you** to sleep over too.
What would you pack for the sleepover?
What games would you play?
Write and draw your story!